Whose dinner?

First published in Great Britain 1988
by Octopus Publishing Group for
The Parent and Child Programme
Published 1997 by Mammoth
an imprint of Reed International Books Limited
Michelin House, 81 Fulham Road, London, SW3 6RB
and Auckland, Melbourne, Singapore and Toronto

10 9 8 7 6 5 4 3 2 1

Copyright © Reed International Books Limited 1988

0 7497 3013 7

A CIP catalogue record for this title
is available from the British Library

Produced by Mandarin Offset Ltd
Printed and bound in Hong Kong

Whose dinner?

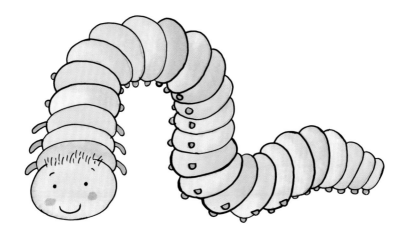

Written and devised by
David Bennett

Illustrated by
Julie Lacome

Here is an acorn from an oak tree.

Whose dinner can it be?

Do you know whose dinner it is?

"Oh yes," says squirrel,
"as you can see,
my dinner is acorns
from an oak tree."

"Hello," says rabbit,
"is it for me?"

"Oh no," says rabbit,
"I like crunching carrots."

"Hello," says sheep,
"is it for me?"

"Oh no," says sheep,
"I like chewing grass."

"Hello," says monkey,
"is it for me?"

"Oh no," says monkey,
"I like gobbling bananas."

"Hello," says caterpillar, "is it for me?"

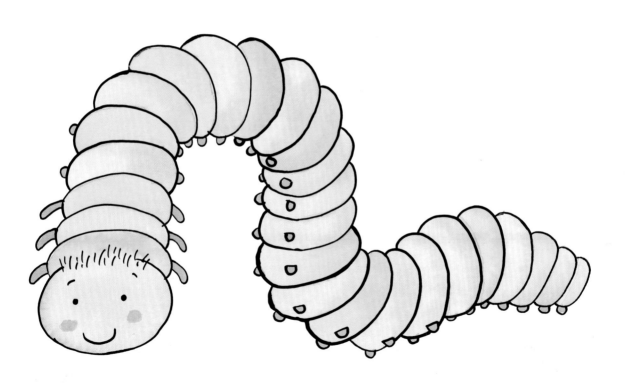

"Oh no," says caterpillar,
"I like nibbling leaves."

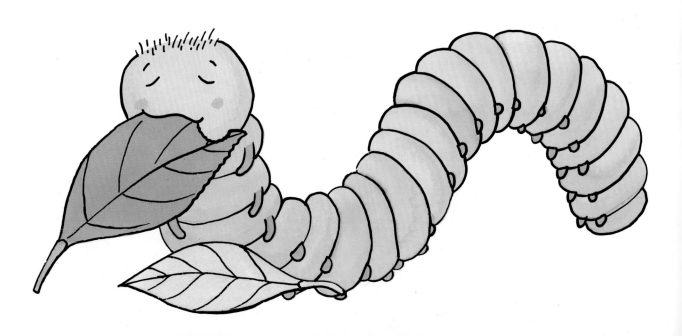

"Hello," says baby,
"is it for me?"

"Oh no," says baby,
"I like eating cereal."

"Hello," says dog,
"is it for me?"

"Oh no," says dog,
"I like biting bones."

"Hello," says hen,
"is it for me?"

"Oh no," says hen,
"I like pecking corn."

"Hello," says panda,
"is it for me?"

"Oh no," says panda,
"I like munching bamboo."